I0671105

Beyond the Door

Beyond the Door

PHILIP K. DICK

ÆGYPAN PRESS

This story from the January 1954 issue of *Fantastic Universe*.

Special thanks to Greg Weeks, Stephen Blundell and the Online Distributed Proofreading Team (hich can be found at http://www.pgdp.net).

Beyond the Door
A publication of
ÆGYPAN PRESS

www.aegypan.com

Did you ever wonder at the lonely life the bird in a cuckoo clock has to lead — that it might possibly love and hate just as easily as a real animal of flesh and blood? Philip Dick used that idea for this brief fantasy tale. We're sure that after reading it you'll give cuckoo clocks more respect.

Larry Thomas bought a cuckoo clock for his wife — without knowing the price he would have to pay.

*T*hat night at the dinner table he brought it out and set it down beside her plate. Doris stared at it, her hand to her mouth. "My God, what is it?" She looked up at him, bright-eyed.

"Well, open it."

Doris tore the ribbon and paper from the square package with her sharp nails, her bosom rising and falling. Larry stood watching her as she lifted the lid. He lit a cigarette and leaned against the wall.

"A cuckoo clock!" Doris cried. "A real old cuckoo clock like my mother had." She turned the clock over and over. "Just like my mother had, when Pete was still alive." Her eyes sparkled with tears.

"It's made in Germany," Larry said. After a moment he added, "Carl got it for me wholesale. He knows some guy in the clock business. Otherwise I wouldn't have —" He stopped.

Doris made a funny little sound.

"I mean, otherwise I wouldn't have been able to afford it." He scowled. "What's the matter with you? You've got your clock, haven't you? Isn't that what you want?"

Doris sat holding onto the clock, her fingers pressed against the brown wood.

"Well," Larry said, "what's the matter?"

He watched in amazement as she leaped up and ran from the room, still clutching the clock. He shook his head. "Never satisfied. They're all that way. Never get enough."

He sat down at the table and finished his meal.

The cuckoo clock was not very large. It was hand-made, however, and there were countless frets on it, little indentations and ornaments scored in the soft wood. Doris sat on the bed drying her eyes and winding the clock. She set the hands by her wristwatch. Presently she carefully moved the hands to two minutes of ten. She carried the clock over to the dresser and propped it up.

Then she sat waiting, her hands twisted together in her lap — waiting for the cuckoo to come out, for the hour to strike.

As she sat she thought about Larry and what he had said. And what she had said, too, for that matter — not that she could be blamed for any of it. After all, she couldn't keep listening to him forever without defending herself; you had to blow your own trumpet in the world.

She touched her handkerchief to her eyes suddenly. Why did he have to say that, about getting it wholesale? Why did he have to spoil it all? If he felt that way he needn't have got it in the first place. She clenched her fists. He was so mean, so damn mean.

But she was glad of the little clock sitting there ticking to itself, with its funny grilled edges and the door. Inside the door was the cuckoo, waiting to come out. Was he listening, his head cocked on one side, listening to hear the clock strike so that he would know to come out?

Did he sleep between hours? Well, she would soon see him: she could ask him. And she would show the clock to Bob. He would love it; Bob loved old things, even old stamps and buttons. He liked to go with her to the stores. Of course, it was a little *awkward*, but Larry had been staying at the office so much, and that helped. If only Larry didn't call up sometimes to —

There was a whirr. The clock shuddered and all at once the door opened. The cuckoo came out, sliding swiftly. He paused and looked around solemnly, scrutinizing her, the room, the furniture.

It was the first time he had seen her, she realized, smiling to herself in pleasure. She stood up, coming toward him shyly. "Go on," she said. "I'm waiting."

The cuckoo opened his bill. He whirred and chirped, quickly, rhythmically. Then, after a moment of contemplation, he retired. And the door snapped shut.

She was delighted. She clapped her hands and spun in a little circle. He was marvelous, perfect! And the way he had looked around, studying her, sizing her up. He liked her; she was certain of it. And she, of course, loved him at once, completely. He was just what she had hoped would come out of the little door.

Doris went to the clock. She bent over the little door, her lips close to the wood. "Do you hear me?" she whispered. "I think you're the most wonderful cuckoo in the world." She paused, embarrassed. "I hope you'll like it here."

Then she went downstairs again, slowly, her head high.

Larry and the cuckoo clock really never got along well from the start. Doris said it was because he didn't wind it right, and it didn't like being only half-wound all the time. Larry turned the job of winding over to her; the cuckoo came out every quarter hour and ran the spring down without remorse, and someone had to be ever after it, winding it up again.

Doris did her best, but she forgot a good deal of the time. Then Larry would throw his newspaper down with an elaborate weary motion and stand up. He would go into the dining room where the clock was mounted on the wall over the fireplace. He would take the clock down and making sure that he had his thumb over the little door, he would wind it up.

"Why do you put your thumb over the door?" Doris asked once.

"You're supposed to."

She raised an eyebrow. "Are you sure? I wonder if it isn't that you don't want him to come out while you're standing so close."

"Why not?"

"Maybe you're afraid of him."

Larry laughed. He put the clock back on the wall and gingerly removed his thumb. When Doris wasn't looking he examined his thumb.

There was still a trace of the nick cut out of the soft part of it. Who — or what — had pecked at him?

One Saturday morning, when Larry was down at the office working over some important special accounts, Bob Chambers came to the front porch and rang the bell.

Doris was taking a quick shower. She dried herself and slipped into her robe. When she opened the door Bob stepped inside, grinning.

"Hi," he said, looking around.

"It's all right. Larry's at the office."

"Fine." Bob gazed at her slim legs below the hem of the robe. "How nice you look today."

She laughed. "Be careful! Maybe I shouldn't let you in after all."

They looked at one another, half amused half frightened. Presently Bob said, "If you want, I'll —"

"No, for God's sake." She caught hold of his sleeve. "Just get out of the doorway so I can close it. Mrs. Peters across the street, you know."

She closed the door. "And I want to show you something," she said. "You haven't seen it."

He was interested. "An antique? Or what?"

She took his arm, leading him toward the dining room. "You'll love it, Bobby." She stopped, wide-eyed. "I hope you will. You must; you must love it. It means so much to me — *he* means so much."

"He?" Bob frowned. "Who is he?"

Doris laughed. "You're jealous! Come on." A moment later they stood before the clock, looking up at it. "He'll come out in a few minutes. Wait until you see him. I know you two will get along just fine."

"What does Larry think of him?"

"They don't like each other. Sometimes when Larry's here he won't come out. Larry gets mad if he doesn't come out on time. He says —"

"Says what?"

Doris looked down. "He always says he's been robbed, even if he did get it wholesale." She brightened. "But I know he won't come out because he doesn't like Larry. When I'm here alone he comes right out for me, every fifteen minutes, even though he really only has to come out on the hour."

She gazed up at the clock. "He comes out for me because he wants to. We talk; I tell him things. Of course, I'd like to have him upstairs in my room, but it wouldn't be right."

There was the sound of footsteps on the front porch. They looked at each other, horrified.

Larry pushed the front door open, grunting. He set his briefcase down and took off his hat. Then he saw Bob for the first time.

"Chambers. I'll be damned." His eyes narrowed. "What are you doing here?" He came into the dining room. Doris drew her robe about her helplessly, backing away.

"I —" Bob began. "That is, we —" He broke off, glancing at Doris. Suddenly the clock began to whirr. The cuckoo came rushing out, bursting into sound. Larry moved toward him.

"Shut that din off," he said. He raised his fist toward the clock. The cuckoo snapped into silence and retreated. The door closed. "That's better." Larry studied Doris and Bob, standing mutely together.

"I came over to look at the clock," Bob said. "Doris told me that it's a rare antique and that —"

"Nuts. I bought it myself." Larry walked up to him. "Get out of here." He turned to Doris. "You too. And take that damn clock with you."

He paused, rubbing his chin. "No. Leave the clock here. It's mine; I bought it and paid for it."

In the weeks that followed after Doris left, Larry and the cuckoo clock got along even worse than before. For one thing, the cuckoo stayed inside most of the time, sometimes even at twelve o'clock when he should have been busiest. And if he did come out at all he usually spoke only once or twice, never the correct number of times. And there was a sullen, uncooperative note in his voice, a jarring sound that made Larry uneasy and a little angry.

But he kept the clock wound, because the house was very still and quiet and it got on his nerves not to hear someone running around, talking and dropping things. And even the whirring of a clock sounded good to him.

But he didn't like the cuckoo at all. And sometimes he spoke to him.

"Listen," he said late one night to the closed little door. "I know you can hear me. I ought to give you back to the Germans — back to the Black Forest." He paced back and forth. "I wonder what they're doing now, the two of them. That young punk with his books and his antiques. A man shouldn't be interested in antiques; that's for women."

He set his jaw. "Isn't that right?"

The clock said nothing. Larry walked up in front of it. "Isn't that right?" he demanded. "Don't you have anything to say?"

He looked at the face of the clock. It was almost eleven, just a few seconds before the hour. "All right. I'll wait until eleven. Then I want to hear what you have to say. You've been pretty quiet the last few weeks since she left."

He grinned wryly. "Maybe you don't like it here since she's gone." He scowled. "Well, I paid for you, and you're coming out whether you like it or not. You hear me?"

Eleven o'clock came. Far off, at the end of town, the great tower clock boomed sleepily to itself. But the little door remained shut. Nothing moved. The minute hand passed on and the cuckoo did not stir. He was someplace inside the clock, beyond the door, silent and remote.

"All right, if that's the way you feel," Larry murmured, his lips twisting. "But it isn't fair. It's your job to come out. We all have to do things we don't like."

He went unhappily into the kitchen and opened the great gleaming refrigerator. As he poured himself a drink he thought about the clock.

There was no doubt about it — the cuckoo should come out, Doris or no Doris. He had always liked her, from the very start. They had got along well, the two of them. Probably he liked Bob too — probably he had seen enough of Bob to get to know him. They would be quite happy together, Bob and Doris and the cuckoo.

Larry finished his drink. He opened the drawer at the sink and took out the hammer. He carried it carefully into the dining room. The clock was ticking gently to itself on the wall.

"Look," he said, waving the hammer. "You know what I have here? You know what I'm going to do with it? I'm going to start on you — first." He smiled. "Birds of a feather, that's what you are — the three of you."

The room was silent.

"Are you coming out? Or do I have to come in and get you?"

The clock whirred a little.

"I hear you in there. You've got a lot of talking to do, enough for the last three weeks. As I figure it, you owe me —"

The door opened. The cuckoo came out fast, straight at him. Larry was looking down, his brow wrinkled in thought. He glanced up, and the cuckoo caught him squarely in the eye.

Down he went, hammer and chair and everything, hitting the floor with a tremendous crash. For a moment the cuckoo paused, its small body poised rigidly. Then it went back inside its house. The door snapped tight-shut after it.

The man lay on the floor, stretched out grotesquely, his head bent over to one side. Nothing moved or stirred. The room was completely silent, except, of course, for the ticking of the clock.

"I see," Doris said, her face tight. Bob put his arm around her, steadying her.

"Doctor," Bob said, "can I ask you something?"

"Of course," the doctor said.

"Is it very easy to break your neck, falling from so low a chair? It wasn't very far to fall. I wonder if it might not have been an accident. Is there any chance it might have been —"

"Suicide?" the doctor rubbed his jaw. "I never heard of anyone committing suicide that way. It was an accident; I'm positive."

"I don't mean suicide," Bob murmured under his breath, looking up at the clock on the wall. "I meant *something else.*"

But no one heard him.